To
Ben

A remembrance of
our many times together
reading this book at the
Nature Museum — I love
you very much — "Mis." Pat

# Quiet Night

by **Marilyn Singer**

illustrated by **John Manders**

CLARION BOOKS / NEW YORK

Clarion Books
a Houghton Mifflin Company imprint
215 Park Avenue South, New York, NY 10003

Text copyright © 2002 by Marilyn Singer
Illustrations copyright © 2002 by John Manders

The illustrations were painted on Arches hot press watercolor paper using
Winsor & Newton gouache and Prismacolor pencils.

www.houghtonmifflinbooks.com

Printed in Singapore

Library of Congress Cataloging-in-Publication Data
Singer, Marilyn.
Quiet night / by Marilyn Singer ; illustrated by John Manders.
p. cm.
Summary: One frog, two owls, three geese are joined by increasingly larger numbers of
different animals that keep ten campers from falling asleep in their tent.
ISBN: 0-618-12044-0
[1. Animal sounds—Fiction. 2. Camping—Fiction. 3. Night—Fiction. 4. Counting.] I. Title
PZ7.S6172 Qu        2002        2001023098
[E] 21

TWP 10 9 8 7 6 5 4 3

To Elizabeth, Ernest, Becca & Honey
& their not-so-quiet nights on Berkeley Place
—M. S.

To Lisa
—J. M.

The moon is big. The moon is bright.

A frog bar-rums on a quiet night.

The trees are black. The grass is white.

Two owls whoo-hoo,
A frog bar-rums on a quiet night.

**The shadows swoop as birds take flight.**

Three geese honk-honk,
Two owls whoo-hoo,
A frog bar-rums on a quiet night.

The lake is calm—no boats in sight.

Four fish whap-slap,
Three geese honk-honk,
Two owls whoo-hoo,
A frog bar-rums on a quiet night.

Who's howling there in sheer delight?

Five coyotes rowl-yowl,
Four fish whap-slap,
Three geese honk-honk,
Two owls whoo-hoo,
A frog bar-rums on a quiet night.

## Somebody's got an appetite

Six raccoons churr-rurr,
Five coyotes rowl-yowl,
Four fish whap-slap,
Three geese honk-honk,
Two owls whoo-hoo,
A frog bar-rums on a quiet night.

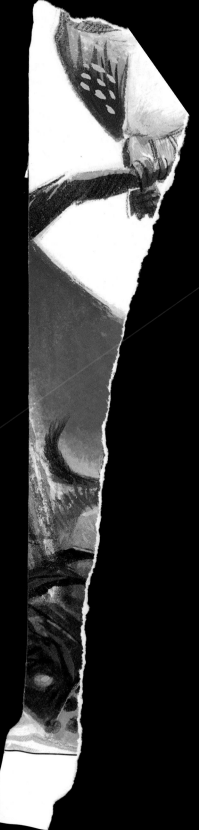

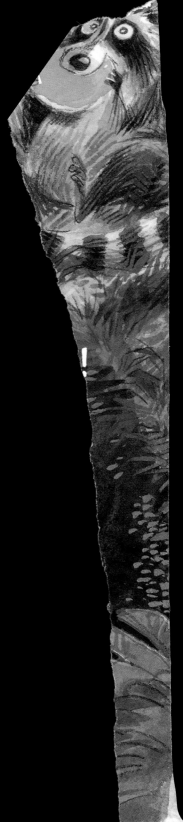

15

# The tent walls twitch. A ghost? A sprite?

Seven mice scritch-scratch,
Six raccoons churr-rurr,
Five coyotes rowl-yowl,
Four fish whap-slap,
Three geese honk-honk,
Two owls whoo-hoo,
A frog bar-rums on a quiet night.

# What's whining here, and will it bite?

Eight mosquitoes eee-eee,
Seven mice scritch-scratch,
Six raccoons churr-rurr,
Five coyotes rowl-yowl,
Four fish whap-slap,
Three geese honk-honk,
Two owls whoo-hoo,
A frog bar-rums on a quiet night.

The forest hums when bugs unite.
Nine crickets chirp-chirp,
Eight mosquitoes eee-eee,
Seven mice scritch-scratch,
Six raccoons churr-rurr,
Five coyotes rowl-yowl,
Four fish whap-slap,
Three geese honk-honk,
Two owls whoo-hoo,
A frog bar-rums on a quiet night.

**Then someone groans, "Turn on the light!"**

Ten campers yawn-yawn,
Nine crickets chirp-chirp,
Eight mosquitoes eee-eee,
Seven mice scritch-scratch,
Six raccoons churr-rurr,
Five coyotes rowl-yowl,
Four fish whap-slap,
Three geese honk-honk,
Two owls whoo-hoo,
A frog bar-rums on a quiet night.

All that stirring, whirring, creeping,

All that whining, all that peeping.

Is there anybody sleeping?

What a NOISY night!